The Legend of the Mystical Book

The Book of Echoes

A Journey Through Time

The Origin of

The Loveday Method®

~

The First in the Series of

Seven Books

A Heptalogy

By

Geoffrey Loveday

MAPLE
PUBLISHERS

The Legend of the Mystical Book: The Book of Echoes

Author: Geoffrey Loveday

Copyright © 2025 Geoffrey Loveday

The right of Geoffrey Loveday to be identified as author of this work has been asserted by the author in accordance with section 77 and 78 of the Copyright, Designs and Patents Act 1988.

First Published in 2025

ISBN 978-1-83538-674-3 (Paperback)
   978-1-83538-675-0 (Hardback)
   978-1-83538-676-7 (E-Book)

Book cover designed and layout by: Geoffrey Loveday

Published by:
   Maple Publishers
   Fairbourne Drive, Atterbury,
   Milton Keynes,
   MK10 9RG, UK
   www.maplepublishers.com

I wonder where life will take us now ...

And so, the journey begins.

Let me take you on this magical adventure.

Contents

Introduction 9

   The Odyssey of Geoffrey Loveday 9

Dedication 11

Inspiration.. 15

The Loveday Method® 18

The Legend of the Mystical Book 19

Breaking the Cycle... 19

The Book of Echoes 21

   Chapter One: Whispers in the Dark 21

   Chapter Two: The Ink of Time 22

   Chapter Three: The First Life............................. 24

   Chapter Four: The Wound Beneath the Skin........ 27

   Chapter Five: Awakening.................................... 29

   Chapter Six: The Next Passage 30

   Chapter Seven: The Physician's Hands................. 31

   Chapter Eight: The Others Who Follow 33

   Epilogue: The First Seeker................................. 34

The Loveday Method and the Seekers of Time 36

   Chapter Nine: The First Seeker's Descent 36

   Chapter Ten: A Life in the Water 38

   Chapter Eleven: The Release 39

   Chapter Twelve: The Others Who Come 40

   Chapter Thirteen: The Guardian of the Book........ 41

Origins of the Book & the Web of Journeys 43

Chapter Fourteen: The First Scribe 43

Chapter Fifteen: The Birth of the Book 44

Chapter Sixteen: The Threads of Many Lives 46

Epilogue: The Next Guardian 48

The Echoes of Sir Roland 54

Echoes in the Present 58

A New Purpose 61

Echoes of Healing 62

The Healer's Burden 63

A Path Forward 65

Echoes That Heal 67

The Third Seeker: A Leader's Doubt 68

The Chief's Trial 69

Returning With Clarity 72

The Fourth Seeker: An Artist's Block 74

The Artisan's Rebellion 75

The Canvas Speaks Again 77

Echoes of Transformation 78

The Book of Echoes Finds Another Way 80

Chapter Seventeen: The Forgotten Name 80

Chapter Eighteen: The Bookshop on Fleet Street . 81

Chapter Nineteen: A Life Once Lived 83

Chapter Twenty: The Buried Past 84

Chapter Twenty-One: The Guardian's Choice 86

A New Seeker; A Different Time 89

Chapter Twenty-Two: The Astronaut and the Book
.... 89

Chapter Twenty-Three: The Artifact 90

Chapter Twenty-Four: The Fall Through Memory 91

Chapter Twenty-Five: The Soldier He Once Was .. 92

Chapter Twenty-Six: The Choice That Was Never
Made 94

Chapter Twenty-Seven: The Awakening 96

Epilogue: The Next Guardian 97

Another Seeker, Another Time 99

Chapter Twenty-Eight: The Samurai and the Book
.... 99

Chapter Twenty-Nine: The Warrior She Once Was
.... 100

Chapter Thirty: The Last Stand 101

Chapter Thirty-One: Breaking the Cycle 103

Chapter Thirty-Two: The Return 104

Chapter Thirty-Three: The Path of the Book 105

A New Seeker in the Industrial Age 106

Chapter Thirty-Four: The Engineer and the Book
.... 106

Chapter Thirty-Five: The Weaver's Tale 107

Chapter Thirty-Six: Embracing Transformation. 108

Epilogue: The Ever-Turning Wheel 109

A New Seeker in the Digital Revolution 110

Chapter Thirty-seven: The Programmer and the Book 110

Chapter Thirty-eight: The Telegraph Operator's Dilemma 111

Chapter Thirty-nine: Embracing Change 112

Epilogue: The Ever-Turning Wheel 113

Chapter forty: The Spy and the Book 113

Chapter Forty-One: A Life He Shouldn't Remember 115

Chapter Forty-Two: The Guillotine's Shadow 116

Chapter Forty-Three: The Message Across Time 117

Chapter Forty-Four: The Spy's Next Move 118

Julian's Race Against Time 120

Chapter Forty-Five: The Web of Deceit 120

Chapter Forty-Six: The Confrontation 121

Chapter Forty-Seven: The Revelation 123

Chapter Forty-Eight: The Aftermath 123

A New Seeker in the Age of Exploration 125

Chapter Forty-Nine: The Navigator and the Book 125

Chapter Fifty: The Viking's Voyage 126

Chapter Fifty-One: The Return 128

Chapter Fifty-Two: The Philosopher's Revelation 129

Chapter Fifty-Three The Alchemist's Journey 130

Chapter Fifty-four: The Enlightened Path 131

Chapter Fifty-Five: The Patriot's Awakening 132

Chapter Fifty-Six: The Spartan's Trial 134

Chapter Fifty-Seven: The Midnight Ride 135

Chapter Fifty-Eight: The Guardian's Revelation 136

Chapter Fifty-Nine: The Awakening 138

Chapter Sixty: The Ancestral Memory 139

Chapter Sixty-One: The Revelation 140

A Meeting Across Time 142

Chapter Sixty-Two: The Convergence 142

Chapter Sixty-Three the Dialogue Beyond Time. 143

Chapter Sixty-Four: The Parting Gift 145

The Book of Echoes, ... 147

Ancient Mystical Book 148

This Is Just the Beginning 151

Beyond Time: The Power to Revisit, Rewrite, and
Heal 153

Introduction

The Odyssey of Geoffrey Loveday

As Geoffrey Elliott Loveday, a professional hypnotherapist, hypnoanalyst, and certified hypnosis instructor Author of eight books, I have dedicated my career to exploring the depths of the human mind and facilitating healing through innovative techniques. My journey led me to develop The Loveday Method, a therapeutic approach that emerged from a profound dream, guiding clients to relive past lives and uncover emotions affecting their present well-being.

The Loveday Method is designed to take clients on a temporal journey, allowing them to experience lives lived long before their current existence. By accessing these deep-seated memories, individuals can identify and address emotional residues that manifest as challenges in their present lives. This process not only provides insight but also facilitates profound healing, enabling clients to release burdens they may have unconsciously carried across lifetimes.

Through my work, I have witnessed the transformative power of this method, as clients gain clarity, resolve deep-rooted issues, and achieve a sense of inner peace. The narratives and journeys presented in my writings aim to illustrate the profound impact of The Loveday Method, offering readers a glimpse into the possibilities of healing and self-discovery that lie within.

The Loveday Method® stands as a testament to the profound connections between our past and present selves, offering a pathway to healing that transcends time and fosters holistic well-being.

Dedication

This book is a tribute to the extraordinary souls who have shaped my life, leaving an indelible mark on my heart. Their love, wisdom, and unwavering support have been my foundation, guiding me through every triumph and trial. I honour them here, with gratitude that words can scarcely contain.

Each day, I carry the memory of my father; a presence so strong, so steady, that even in his absence, he remains a guiding force in my life. His love and wisdom shaped me in ways too numerous to count, and now, in the silence left behind, I feel an ache that never truly fades. Yet, in that ache, there is love; enduring, unbreakable.

First and foremost, I dedicate this book to the memory of my beloved mother. Our time together was heartbreakingly brief, yet her spirit lives within me, shaping my days and filling my heart with the love she left behind. Her absence taught me the preciousness of time, the importance of cherishing every fleeting moment. And though she is gone, her presence is felt in the quiet strength she instilled in me.

I have been blessed beyond measure to be nurtured by the wisdom and kindness of my grandparents, aunts, and uncles. Their lessons, built on love and experience, have been a compass in my life, illuminating my path and reminding me always of the legacy I carry forward. Their love is a quiet strength that sustains me still.

To my in-laws, Alma and Leon · your love has been a gift I never take for granted. You welcomed me as your own, offering warmth, acceptance, and an unwavering sense of family. For that, I am forever grateful.

To my dear wife, whose absence I feel deeply as I watch our children grow · your love continues to be my guiding light. Your unwavering faith in me, your strength, your gentle encouragement; they still live within me, giving me the courage to face each day. You are forever in my heart.

To our incredible children - you are my greatest source of joy, my deepest well of inspiration. Your strength, love, and unbreakable spirit remind me daily of the boundless possibilities that exist, even in life's darkest moments. You are proof of the resilience and love that bind us all.

To my beautiful grandchildren - your laughter, your curiosity, your wonder for the world fills my heart with joy. You are the future of our family, carrying forward the love, the values, and the legacy of those who came before you. In you, I see hope.

To my wonderful sons-in-law - you are not just part of our family; you are family. Your love, your kindness, and the respect you show have only strengthened our bonds. For that, I am deeply grateful.

I also hold close the memory of my cherished brothers. Your absence has left a void that can never be filled, yet your strength, your perseverance, and your unwavering spirit remain with me, guiding me, inspiring me. Though we are separated, you are never truly gone.

And to the many friends, mentors, and supporters who have walked beside me on this journey—your belief in me, your encouragement, your unwavering support have helped bring this book to life. Your kindness has been a light in my darkest hours, and for that, I thank you.

This book is for all who have touched my life—past and present. Your love, your influence, your presence has shaped me in ways I could never fully express. From the depths of my heart, I am endlessly grateful.

Thank you.

Inspiration

I would like to extend my heartfelt gratitude to the incredible individuals who have demonstrated immense courage in battling various illnesses. Your strength and determination have not only inspired me but countless others around the world.

To the fighters, survivors, and those still in the midst of their health challenges, thank you for sharing your stories and experiences. Your resilience has shown us the power of the human spirit and the importance of never giving up.

I am deeply grateful to the healthcare professionals and researchers who tirelessly dedicate themselves to the pursuit of finding better treatments and cures. Your commitment to improving the lives of those affected by illness is truly commendable.

I would also like to acknowledge the unwavering support and love provided by family, friends, and caregivers. Your presence, encouragement, and understanding have been instrumental in my own journey and the creation of this book.

To the organisations and foundations that tirelessly work towards raising awareness, providing resources, and supporting those in need, thank you for your invaluable contributions. Your efforts make a significant difference in the lives of individuals and families facing health challenges.

I am indebted to the readers and supporters of this book, who have shown immense compassion and empathy. Your willingness to listen, learn, and extend a helping hand fosters a sense of community and solidarity in the face of adversity.

Lastly, I would like to express my deep appreciation to my mentors, editors, and everyone involved in the publication of this book. Your guidance, expertise, and belief in this project have been vital in bringing it to fruition.

This book stands as a tribute to the indomitable spirit of those who confront illness with courage. Your stories, struggles, and triumphs have touched my heart and ignited a passion to spread awareness and offer support to those in need.

Thank you, one and all, for your strength, inspiration, and the profound impact you have made on my life and the lives of countless others.

The Loveday Method®

"Embark on a Journey of Mastery and understanding"

This book is more than mere words on a page; it's a portal, a gateway through time and possibility. Within these pages, you won't just read stories; you will live them. These journeys aren't confined to fiction; they pulse with truth, waiting to unfold in the depths of your imagination. Every adventure, every revelation, is as real as you choose to make it.

You can travel anywhere; across distant worlds, through forgotten histories, or into the deepest corners of the human soul. The only limit is your belief. Trust in yourself, open your mind, and step beyond the ordinary.

Let the impossible become real.

The Legend of the Mystical Book

Breaking the Cycle

Whispers of an ancient legend speak of a book unlike any other—one not crafted with ink nor bound by mortal hands, but etched upon the very fabric of time itself. It is said that those who find it do not merely read its pages; they step into them, slipping through the veils of the past to walk paths long forgotten.

This is no ordinary chronicle of history. The book does not recount the deeds of kings or the rise and fall of empires. Instead, it reveals the hidden echoes of one's own soul—reliving the moments that shaped them before they even drew breath. It is a mirror, reflecting the silent wounds carried across lifetimes, unravelling the unseen threads that weave through one's pain, one's joys, and one's fate.

And yet, no temple has ever held it, no scholar has ever turned its pages. As the centuries passed, the greatest minds of every age came to question its very existence. Perhaps, they mused, it was never meant to be found in the physical world at all. Perhaps it was not a book, but a key—one that unlocks the boundless corridors of the mind, where time is not a river but an ocean, limitless and ever-reaching.

Still, the seekers remain. Not searching in dusty ruins or buried tombs, but within—the only place the book has ever truly existed. For those who dare to look, the past and present are but two halves of the same whole, and in their convergence lies the power to heal—not only oneself, but all of humanity.

And so, the search continues. Will you dare to open the book? Will you step beyond time and face the truths long hidden within its pages?

The journey awaits.

The Book of Echoes

Chapter One: Whispers in the Dark

The wind carried the scent of rain as Elias stepped into the crumbling ruins of what had once been a temple. Moonlight slanted through the broken columns, bathing the ancient stone in silver. The silence here was thick, pressing against his ears like the hush before a storm.

He had spent years chasing a legend—a story so old, so buried in myth, that most had forgotten it ever existed. But Elias had not. For as long as he could remember, the whispers had haunted him, slipping into his dreams, speaking in voices that were not his own.

The book is not found. The book is remembered.

That was what the elders had told him when he first began his search. At the time, he had dismissed their words as riddles, the ramblings of those who had long since abandoned the quest. But now, standing here, he felt it—an undeniable pull, as though something just beyond the veil of reality was waiting. Watching.

He ran his fingers along the ancient carvings on the temple wall. They were smooth, worn by centuries of wind and rain, yet beneath his touch, they burned. Images flashed behind his eyes—shadows moving through time, flickering like candlelight. He staggered back, heart pounding.

This was no ordinary legend. This was a doorway.

Chapter Two: The Ink of Time

Elias awoke to darkness. Not the absence of light, but a deep, endless void, stretching beyond his sight. He was no longer in the temple. He was nowhere.

The voices returned, murmuring just beyond his comprehension. They swirled around him like a wind that carried no air.

"Who are you?"

The question was not spoken aloud, yet it echoed inside him.

"I—I don't know," Elias whispered.

A flicker of light appeared before him, swirling like ink dropped into water. It took shape—pages fluttering, letters shifting. A book, ancient and bound in leather that pulsed as though alive.

"Then read."

His hands trembled as he reached for it. The moment his fingers brushed the cover, the world shattered.

He fell.

Through time, through memory, through lifetimes not his own.

And the book—his book—began to write itself in the ink of his soul.

Chapter Three: The First Life

Elias hit the ground with a force that rattled his bones. He gasped, sucking in air that smelled of salt and fire. The world around him spun, shifting like the surface of water disturbed by a stone.

When the dizziness passed, he found himself standing on the edge of a vast desert. The sky overhead bled gold and crimson, the sun dipping toward the horizon. But this was no place he had ever seen before. The dunes stretched endlessly, and in the distance, black stone pyramids rose against the dying light.

He turned sharply at the sound of voices. A group of figures moved toward him, cloaked in flowing robes, their faces obscured by hoods. They spoke in a tongue Elias did not recognize, yet somehow, he understood.

"He has come."

"The echoes have awakened."

Elias stepped back, his pulse roaring in his ears. "Who are you?" he demanded, though his voice trembled.

One of the figures lowered their hood, revealing the face of a woman—ageless, yet worn by time. Her eyes were dark as the void he had fallen through, but filled with something deeper than knowledge.

"You are not here by accident, traveller," she said. "You are here because you have always been here."

The words sent a shiver through him. He looked down at his hands—only they were not his hands. The skin was darker, the fingers calloused from labour. He reached for his reflection in the shallow water pooled between the rocks.

The face that stared back was not his own.

Panic clenched his chest. "What is this?"

The woman stepped forward; her expression unreadable. "You are reliving what has been forgotten. The book does not show you what you wish to see. It shows you what you must remember."

Memories that were not his own rushed through his mind—flashes of laughter, the weight of a sword in his hand, the scent of burning incense in a temple long turned to dust. He knew this life. He had lived it.

"You must find the wound," the woman said. "Only then can you return."

Elias turned to her, desperate. "How do I wake up?"

She smiled, a sad, knowing smile. "You do not wake up. You remember. Only when you understand the pain of this life can you heal the one you left behind."

And then the world blurred again.

Chapter Four: The Wound Beneath the Skin

Elias stood in a dimly lit chamber. Torches flickered against the stone walls, illuminating a figure kneeling before him. His heart pounded as he took an unconscious step forward.

He recognized this moment. It was a memory—a memory belonging to the man whose body he now inhabited.

The kneeling man was whispering words of mercy. His wrists were bound, his face bloodied. And in Elias's own hand, a dagger gleamed.

He knew what came next. He was the executioner.

A sharp pain tore through his chest, as if something ancient and broken was clawing its way to the surface.

This was the wound.

Not a scar on his skin, but on his soul. The choice he had made in this life—perhaps unwillingly, perhaps out of duty—had left an imprint so deep that even lifetimes later, it lingered.

The book had brought him here to face it.

Elias clenched his jaw, his breath ragged. He had no memory of who this man was, or why he had been sentenced to death. But it didn't matter. What mattered was the guilt—the weight he had carried across time, never knowing its source.

He lowered the dagger. The kneeling man looked up, eyes widening in shock.

"You choose a different path," the voice whispered.

A sudden force pulled Elias backward. The world cracked apart once more, and he felt himself spiralling, falling through darkness—until, at last, he hit the ground once more

Chapter Five: Awakening

Elias's eyes flew open. He was back.

The ruins surrounded him, silent and cold, just as he had left them. The ancient carvings beneath his fingers no longer burned. His heart pounded as he struggled to his feet, his breath uneven.

But something was different. The weight in his chest—the hollow, aching void he had carried his entire life—was gone.

He knew now.

The book was not an object to be found. It was a doorway, a mirror, a key to the past that had always lived within him. It did not simply reveal history— it revealed the scars of the soul, the unhealed wounds that shaped the present.

He had relived his first life.

And there would be others.

Elias turned, the wind stirring the dust at his feet. Somewhere beyond this place, beyond this moment, the book still called to him.

Because the past was not done with him yet. And neither was the journey.

Chapter Six: The Next Passage

Elias stood at the threshold of time, no longer questioning how or why the book had chosen him. The knowledge pulsed within him—this was not just his journey. He was merely the first. Others would come after him, seekers drawn by wounds they could not name, guided by the echoes of lives long past.

But he had to master it first.

The air around him shifted, the ruins blurring once more as the invisible hand of the book pulled him forward. His pulse quickened. This time, he did not resist.

As the world unravelled, Elias stepped willingly into the abyss.

Chapter Seven: The Physician's Hands

Elias landed hard, dust rising around him in a swirl. He blinked, adjusting to the dim candlelight of what appeared to be an old study. Shelves of aged manuscripts lined the walls, and the scent of herbs filled the air.

He caught his reflection in a polished brass mirror. His face was no longer his own—it was older, lined with wisdom and sorrow. His hands, strong and veined, bore the marks of someone who had spent a lifetime in healing.

He was a physician.

A knock at the door startled him. A woman entered, her face pale with worry.

"Master Loveday, he is fading fast. You must come at once."

The name sent a jolt through him. Loveday. The name felt familiar, yet foreign, as if it carried weight beyond this life.

He followed the woman down a stone corridor, his feet moving on instinct. Through another door, into a room where a man lay unconscious, his breaths shallow. The others in the room looked to Elias—no, to Loveday—with desperate hope.

Elias understood then. In this life, he had been a healer. A man devoted to understanding the wounds of the body, but more than that—one who had sought to heal wounds of the soul.

The book had brought him here for a reason.

He touched the dying man's hand. And in that moment, visions flooded his mind—flashes of trauma, grief, the burdens that had weakened this man beyond the physical. He saw the threads of pain that stretched across lifetimes.

This was it. This was the key.

Healing was not just about the present—it was about untangling the wounds of the past.

The Loveday Method was more than medicine. It was a bridge between time and self.

And now, Elias understood why he had been chosen.

Chapter Eight: The Others Who Follow

When Elias awoke again in the ruins, his body trembled, but his mind burned with clarity. The book had not just been showing him his past—it had been showing him a method, a path for others to follow.

He had healed something in himself. But now, he had the knowledge to help others do the same.

He was not the only one who needed this.

Word of the book would spread. Those who felt lost, those haunted by invisible pain, would seek him out. And when they came, he would guide them as the book had guided him.

The past was a wound. But it was also a cure.

And so, the Loveday Method was born—not just as a technique, but as a path through time, a way to reach into the echoes of the past and mend what had been broken.

The book was no longer just his burden. It was his gift. And soon, others would read its pages too.

Epilogue: The First Seeker

The first came at dusk, just as Elias knew they would. A woman, eyes dark with questions, stood at the edge of the ruins. She did not speak, but Elias could see it in her face—she carried the echoes too.

Without a word, he placed his hand over hers. The book whispered between them. And her journey began.

The Loveday Method and the Seekers of Time

Chapter Nine: The First Seeker's Descent

Elias watched the woman hesitate at the threshold of the ruins. The weight in her eyes was familiar—the look of someone burdened by something she could not name, haunted by a past she did not remember.

"You've felt it, haven't you?" Elias said, his voice calm but certain.

She nodded. "I don't know why I came here. Only that I had to."

Elias gestured for her to sit beside the flickering fire he had built in the centre of the ruins. He studied her for a moment. The book had not brought just anyone—it had chosen her.

"Tell me what you feel," he said.

She wrapped her arms around herself. "I don't know how to explain it. My whole life, I've had these... moments. Flashes of places I've never been. A fear of water, though I've never drowned. A pain in my chest, though no doctor can find anything wrong." She exhaled sharply. "It's like my soul remembers something my mind doesn't."

Elias nodded. "Then you're ready."

He reached out, placing his fingertips against her wrist. The moment he made contact, a pulse of energy rippled between them.

The book stirred.

She gasped, her eyes widening as the firelight dimmed, the world around them beginning to dissolve.

"Don't fight it," Elias murmured. "Let it show you."

The ruins faded, and the woman fell into the past.

Chapter Ten: A Life in the Water

The world was cold.

She opened her eyes to find herself on the deck of a wooden ship, the scent of salt thick in the air. The ocean roared beneath her feet, waves crashing violently against the hull.

She knew this place.

Though she had never seen it before, her body remembered. The weight of the ropes in her hands, the way the wind stung her cheeks—she had been here once.

"The storm is coming," a voice called behind her.

She turned to see a man—tall, broad-shouldered, with the look of someone who had spent a lifetime battling the sea.

And suddenly, she remembered.

He was her husband. And this was the night they were going to die.

The storm had come swiftly, swallowing their ship in its fury. She had drowned here, in these waters, the taste of salt burning her throat, her screams lost in the wind.

That was why, in this life, she feared the water. That was why the pain in her chest had never left.

Because she had never let go.

Chapter Eleven: The Release

Back in the ruins, Elias watched as she gasped, her body shaking, tears streaming down her face.

"It wasn't just a dream," she whispered. "It was real."

Elias nodded. "It was real once. But it does not have to be real now."

She clutched at her chest, breathing hard. "I never forgave myself. I tried to save him. I couldn't."

"You carried the guilt across lifetimes," Elias said gently. "But now you know. And now, you can release it."

She closed her eyes, inhaling deeply. And as she exhaled, the weight lifted.

The fear, the pain—it faded.

When she opened her eyes again, she was free.

The first healing was complete.

Chapter Twelve: The Others Who Come

Word spread. The first seeker became two, then five, then ten. Each came with an ache they could not explain—a fear, a sorrow, a wound deeper than flesh.

And one by one, Elias guided them.

A warrior who had lived a hundred battles, carrying guilt for the lives he had taken.

A woman who had always felt unseen, unaware that she had once been silenced by the hands of a tyrant.

A child who had been born screaming, afraid of the dark, not knowing that in another life, he had died alone in a prison cell.

Each journey through time unravelled the unseen wounds they carried.

Each healing rippled across lifetimes.

The Loveday Method was no longer just Elias's knowledge—it belonged to all who sought it.

Chapter Thirteen: The Guardian of the Book

Elias knew the book had chosen him for a reason.

He was not just its reader.

He was its guardian.

But something deeper called to him—something beyond himself, beyond even the seekers.

There was one final mystery the book had yet to reveal.

Who wrote it?

And why had it been left behind?

He could feel it now, whispering just beyond the edge of his understanding.

His journey was not over.

It was just beginning.

Origins of the Book & the Web of Journeys

Chapter Fourteen: The First Scribe

Elias had spent years guiding others through the Loveday Method, uncovering the wounds that stretched across lifetimes. Yet one mystery remained—the book itself.

It had appeared to him when he was ready; whispered its truths, and revealed the echoes of time. But where had it come from? Who had written it?

The answers lay within the book itself.

So, one night, beneath the silver glow of the moon, Elias placed his hands upon its cover and allowed it to take him back—not just into his own past, but to the first hands that ever held it.

The world fractured.

And when it reassembled, Elias found himself standing in the heart of an ancient temple, where a figure sat hunched over a stone slab, carving symbols into its surface.

The first scribe.

Chapter Fifteen: The Birth of the Book

The scribe was a woman, her robes threadbare, her fingers stained with ink. Elias knew, without being told, that she was the one who had first inscribed the book into existence.

And she was dying.

Her breaths were shallow, her body frail, yet she continued to carve, etching each letter with the weight of a thousand souls.

Elias stepped forward, though he knew she could not see him. He was only an observer here—a shadow in time.

"Why do you write?" he whispered, though no sound left his lips.

As if in answer, the woman murmured to herself, her voice weak but determined.

"Time is not a river. It is a circle. The wounds of one life become the echoes of another. This book must endure, so that those who come after me will remember."

Her chisel scraped against stone, and Elias saw the words forming beneath her hands.

"The soul does not forget. But the mind does. This book is the key to remembering."

A realization struck him like lightning; the book had never been written in ink. It had been written in time itself.

Each name, each passage, was a record of lives lost and found, wounds inflicted and healed.

This woman—this ancient scribe—had not created the book. She had merely been its first guardian, just as Elias was now.

And as she placed her trembling hands upon the stone tablet, a golden light pulsed from its surface, spreading outward in ripples through time.

The book had been born. Not as a physical object, but as a living force. It would appear whenever it was needed, to whoever was ready to see.

And now, Elias knew. He was not the first. And he would not be the last.

Chapter Sixteen: The Threads of Many Lives

Elias awoke with a sharp gasp, the ruins of the temple solidifying around him once more. His pulse pounded, but his mind was clear.

The book had existed for centuries. It had passed from one seeker to another, each of them unlocking its secrets in their own way.

And now, those who had been healed by the Loveday Method would soon discover—they, too, had a role to play.

The book did not belong to one person.

It belonged to all who sought to remember.

And across the world, across time, others were beginning to hear its call.

A young scholar in India, waking from dreams of a life she had never lived.

A warrior in the highlands of Scotland, feeling the echoes of battles fought before his birth.

A lost soul in the streets of New York, drawn to a bookshop where a certain ancient manuscript waited.

The journeys were many. The wounds were deep. But the book had always been there. Waiting. And Elias was ready to guide them.

Epilogue: The Next Guardian

One day, the book would leave him.

Elias understood this now. Just as the first scribe had passed it down through time, just as he had been chosen when the moment was right—soon, another would take his place.

But not yet. For now, the book was his to protect, his to share. He had begun as a seeker. Now, he was the guardian.

And the book... The book would live on.

Elias stood at the threshold of a new era, the weight of the Book of Echoes resting gently in his hands. He had always known this moment would come—the time when he would pass the sacred tome to its next guardian. The Book had chosen him, guided him, and now, it was ready to continue its journey through the annals of time.

As he gazed upon the ancient, leather-bound cover, memories of his own journey flooded back. He had begun as a seeker, yearning for knowledge and understanding. The Book had opened his eyes to the interconnectedness of all things, revealing the tapestry of existence woven through countless lives and experiences.

Now, as its guardian, Elias had fulfilled his role, guided others and safeguarding the wisdom contained within its pages. He understood that the Book was not his to keep; it was a living entity, meant to touch the lives of many, to inspire and enlighten across generations.

With a deep breath, Elias placed the Book upon a pedestal bathed in ethereal light. He whispered words of gratitude and farewell, knowing that its next guardian would soon arrive, drawn by the same call that had once beckoned him.

As he stepped back, the room seemed to shimmer, the air thick with anticipation. Elias smiled, a sense of peace washing over him. His journey with the Book had come to an end, but its legacy would endure.

The Book of Echoes would live on, continuing its sacred mission to illuminate the paths of those destined to seek its wisdom.

And Elias, now a part of its eternal story, would forever be connected to the endless chain of seekers and guardians, bound together by the timeless pursuit of knowledge and enlightenment.

In the quiet town of Ashcroft, nestled between rolling hills and ancient forests, lived Clara Bennett, a young historian with an insatiable curiosity for the past. Her days were spent amidst dusty manuscripts and forgotten relics, piecing together stories of those who had come before.

One crisp autumn morning, while exploring a long-abandoned estate on the outskirts of town,

Clara discovered a hidden chamber behind a decaying bookshelf. Within, bathed in a shaft of golden sunlight, lay an ornate, leather-bound tome—the Book of Echoes. Its cover was adorned with intricate symbols that seemed to pulse with a life of their own.

As Clara reached out to touch the book, a warmth spread through her fingertips, and a cascade of visions flooded her mind. She saw glimpses of distant lands, ancient civilizations, and faces both familiar and foreign. Overwhelmed, she withdrew her hand, her heart racing with a mix of fear and exhilaration.

That night, sleep eluded Clara. The images she had seen haunted her thoughts, beckoning her to delve deeper. Unable to resist, she returned to the hidden chamber the next day, determined to uncover the secrets of the mysterious tome.

As days turned into weeks, Clara immersed herself in the Book's pages. Each chapter revealed stories of individuals from different eras, all connected by a common thread—their encounters with the Book of Echoes. She read of Elias, the first Guardian, who had dedicated his life to guiding seekers towards enlightenment. His journey resonated deeply with her, igniting a sense of purpose she had never felt before.

One evening, as Clara pored over a particularly enigmatic passage, the air around her seemed to shimmer. A soft, ethereal glow emanated from the Book, and before her stood a figure draped in robes of light.

Elias: "Greetings, Clara. You have been chosen."

Clara: "Chosen? For what?"

Elias: "To become the next Guardian of the Book of Echoes. Your journey has led you here, and now, the mantle passes to you."

Clara's mind raced. The weight of the responsibility pressed upon her, yet beneath it lay a profound sense of honour and destiny.

Clara: "But why me? I'm just a historian."

Elias: "It is precisely your love for history, your dedication to uncovering truths, which makes you worthy. The Book seeks those who can bridge the past and the present, guiding others towards understanding."

As Elias spoke, Clara felt a surge of clarity. The visions, the discoveries, all led to this moment.

Clara: "I accept. I will protect the Book and share its wisdom."

Elias smiled, a look of pride in his eyes.

Elias: "Remember, Clara, the Book is alive with the stories of countless souls. As its Guardian, you are now a part of this eternal tapestry. Trust in yourself, and in the journey ahead."

With that, Elias faded into the light, leaving Clara alone with the Book. But she no longer felt alone. The legacy of the Guardians before her, and the promise of those yet to come, filled her with unwavering resolve.

And so, in the quiet town of Ashcroft, a new chapter began. Clara Bennett, once a seeker of history, had become the Guardian of the Book of Echoes, entrusted with its timeless wisdom and the countless stories it held within.

As the new Guardian of the Book of Echoes, Clara Bennett embraced her role with a profound sense of purpose. She understood that the Book was not merely a repository of ancient wisdom but a living conduit, connecting souls across time and space. Her mission was clear: to guide seekers toward healing and enlightenment by helping them access the echoes of their ancestral pasts.

The Echoes of Sir Roland

The moment James turned the Book of Echoes to the next page, the words shimmered, shifting and twisting like whispers carried by the wind. A sudden pull, like an unseen force grasping his very soul, yanked him from reality. His breath hitched as the world around him melted into darkness, then flared into blinding light.

When his vision cleared, he was no longer in his living room.

The roar of battle consumed him. Swords clashed. Men screamed. Blood darkened the earth. The weight of heavy Armor pressed on his shoulders, a steel gauntlet encased his hand, gripping a sword that gleamed with fresh crimson.

"Sir Roland!" a soldier cried, panting as he stumbled toward James. "We've pushed them back. The village is ours!"

James blinked. Sir Roland? His mind reeled, but the instinctive knowledge was already there—he was Sir Roland. He knew the voice calling him, the weight of the sword in his grip, the taste of battle on his tongue. It was more than a dream; it was real.

A second knight approached, his armour glinting in the setting sun. Sir Cedric, James realized. A trusted comrade—but also a man of ruthless conviction.

"The commander's orders," Cedric said, voice hard. "Purge the village."

James stiffened. "What?"

Cedric's gaze did not waver. "They harboured our enemy. They must pay the price."

James turned toward the village. Smoke curled from thatched rooftops. Women clutched their children, wide-eyed with terror. A boy—no older than ten—stood frozen, his small hand gripping a wooden sword, a useless defence against the armed knights.

James's pulse pounded. No. This isn't right.

Cedric stepped closer; voice low. "We swore an oath, Roland."

James's throat tightened. He wasn't just a spectator in this memory—he could feel Sir Roland's turmoil, his duty warring against his conscience. Obedience meant safety. Defiance meant disgrace, exile... or death.

The boy locked eyes with him. Fear and desperation swirled within them.

James gritted his teeth. "No."

Cedric's brows furrowed. "What?"

James turned, raising his sword—not against the villagers, but against his own men.

"Stand down," he ordered. "These people are not our enemies."

Gasps rippled through the soldiers. Cedric's eyes darkened. "You would defy the commander?"

"I would defy butchery."

The silence stretched like the pull of a bowstring before release. Then Cedric sneered, stepping back. "Then you are no knight of this order."

James's fate was sealed at that moment. He knew it, felt it in his very bones. The condemnation, the loss of everything he had built—his knighthood, his honour—was now dust in the wind.

But the boy still breathed. The villagers still lived.

And that was enough.

Echoes in the Present

James gasped as reality came rushing back. His fingers clawed at his chest, searching for armour that was no longer there. The weight of the sword was gone, replaced by the cold, familiar silence of his apartment.

But the guilt remained.

He pressed a hand to his forehead, his breath unsteady. He had been Sir Roland. He had felt the crushing weight of his decision, the sting of exile. But more than that—he had felt his atonement.

A knock at the door startled him. Clara's voice followed. "James? You, okay?"

He hesitated, then exhaled slowly. "Yeah... Come in."

She stepped inside, concern etching her features. "You looked like you were in a fight for your life."

James chuckled dryly. "In a way, I was."

She sat across from him, waiting. She always waited, never pushed. That was why he trusted her.

So, for the first time in years, James spoke. Not in half-truths. Not in deflections. He told her everything—about Sir Roland, about the battle, about the choice he had made and the exile that followed.

When he finished, Clara was silent for a long moment. Then she said, "He sounds a lot like you."

James's breath hitched. "What do you mean?"

"You both did what was right, even when it cost you everything." She leaned forward. "You've spent years punishing yourself for choices you made in war, James. But what if your purpose—your redemption—comes from helping others find their own?"

The words struck deep. He had saved those villagers as Sir Roland... but he was still saving people now, wasn't he? Every time he reached out to a fellow veteran, every time he offered an ear, every time he helped someone else find their footing.

The past wasn't a weight meant to drag him down.

It was a guide, leading him forward.

A New Purpose

In the weeks that followed, James felt the shift within him. He spoke at group meetings, shared his story with others who had walked the same path of guilt and self-doubt. He no longer carried the burden alone.

His family noticed the change—the light returning to his eyes, the way he no longer flinched away from their concern. He laughed more. He lived more.

One day, as he placed the Book of Echoes back on the shelf, he ran his fingers along the worn cover. He wasn't sure how it worked, why it had shown him that past life.

But he was grateful.

Because some echoes were not meant to haunt. Some were meant to heal.

And James had finally heard them.

Echoes of Healing

Clara found Elena sitting on the park bench, her gaze fixed on nothing in particular. The woman's face was pale, worn from too many sleepless nights, her fingers twisting the fabric of her coat in restless movements.

Clara approached cautiously. "Elena?"

Elena blinked, as if waking from a dream. "Oh. Clara." Her voice was hoarse, like she hadn't spoken much in days. Maybe weeks.

Clara sat beside her, silent for a moment. The air was thick with unsaid things. Finally, she said, "I know the weight you're carrying."

Elena gave a bitter laugh, shaking her head. "No. You don't."

Clara reached into her bag and pulled out the Book of Echoes. She had been unsure at first,

hesitant to share its power with others. But now…
now, she knew that Elena needed to see.

"Elena," she said softly, placing the book between
them. "Let me show you something."

Elena frowned but hesitated only for a moment
before reaching out. As soon as her fingers touched
the ancient cover, the world shifted.

The Healer's Burden

Elena found herself in a dimly lit cottage, the
scent of herbs and burning incense thick in the air.
A fire crackled in the hearth, casting flickering
shadows across the walls lined with vials, dried
plants, and handwritten scrolls.

But it was the woman at the centre of the room
who caught Elena's breath.

The healer.

She knelt beside a still form, a young girl, her small hand cold in the healer's grasp.

"She was the last of them," a voice whispered.

Elena turned. An old man stood in the doorway, his face lined with sorrow. "The plague has taken them all."

The healer's hands trembled. "I tried," she whispered. "I did everything I could."

Elena could feel it—the weight of helplessness, the soul-crushing despair. The healer had fought, had spent nights grinding herbs, boiling roots, praying to any gods who would listen. But in the end, it had not been enough.

She let out a shuddering breath. "What is the point of my work if I cannot save them?"

The old man stepped closer, resting a hand on her shoulder. "Because there will always be more who need you."

The words settled in the air, lingering.

The healer swallowed. The grief was still there, it would always be there, but it did not have to be a tomb.

Slowly, she stood, wiped her tears, and turned toward the rows of herbs and remedies that lined her walls.

Not for the ones she had lost. But for those she could still save.

A Path Forward

Elena gasped, her body jolting as she was pulled back into the present. She clutched the edges of the bench, her breath uneven, her heart pounding.

Clara waited.

Elena pressed a hand to her chest. "I... I felt it. Her pain. It was like... it was mine."

Clara nodded. "Because it was."

Elena's vision blurred with unshed tears. "She lost them. All of them. And yet... she kept going."

"She found a way to honour them," Clara said gently. "Not by forgetting, not by replacing them, but by using what she had to help others."

Elena swallowed, her fingers curling into fists. "I don't know how."

"You don't have to know yet," Clara assured her. "But maybe... maybe there's a way to take what you've lived through and make something out of it."

Elena closed her eyes. For the first time in months, there was no void.

There was something else.

A possibility. A path.

She turned to Clara, her voice barely a whisper. "Where do I start?"

Clara smiled, reaching for her hand.

"We'll figure it out together."

Echoes That Heal

Days turned into weeks, and Elena's steps were slow at first. Small. She began volunteering at grief support groups, simply listening, being present. Then she started organizing small acts of kindness— sending letters to bereaved parents, donating to children's charities.

Her grief was still there, a companion she would never part with.

But it no longer chained her.

One day, as she placed a single white flower on her child's memorial, she whispered, "I will carry you forward."

And somehow, she knew, deep in her heart—her child's love would echo on in every life she touched.

The Third Seeker: A Leader's Doubt

Marcus sat in Clara's small office, his hands clasped together, fingers drumming restlessly. His broad shoulders, which usually carried the weight of others with ease, now sagged under an invisible burden.

"I don't know if I can do this anymore," he admitted. His voice was steady, but the weariness in his eyes betrayed him.

Clara tilted her head. "What makes you say that?"

He let out a humourless chuckle. "Because I'm failing. I can feel it. Every decision I make feels like a gamble, and I can't shake the fear that one wrong step will bring everything crashing down."

She studied him for a moment, then reached for the Book of Echoes. "Maybe it's not failure you fear," she said gently. "Maybe it's the weight of responsibility."

Marcus frowned as she slid the book toward him. "What is this?"

Clara smiled knowingly. "A perspective you might need."

Hesitantly, Marcus placed his hands on the book. The moment his fingers met the cover, the world blurred.

The Chief's Trial

Marcus blinked and found himself somewhere else.

The scent of rain-soaked earth filled his lungs. The dense jungle around him buzzed with life— chirping insects, distant calls of unseen creatures. A fire burned at the centre of a gathering, casting flickering shadows on a circle of warriors.

He looked down. Fur-lined garments. Hands calloused by labour. A ceremonial pendant carved from bone rested against his chest.

He was the chief.

A voice broke through the murmurs of the gathered warriors.

"The drought has taken the crops. The hunters return empty-handed. The people are afraid."

Marcus turned toward the speaker, an elder with piercing eyes. He felt the weight of those eyes pressing against his soul.

"What will you do, Chief?" another warrior asked.

The question sent a chill through Marcus's spine.

He didn't have an answer. His people waited. Expectant. Trusting.

And yet he doubted.

Would his decision lead them to survival, or to ruin? What if he chose wrong?

His fingers curled into fists. He could not show weakness.

But then...

A voice whispered in his mind, echoing from the depths of the Book.

Doubt is not a weakness. The realization struck him as if the earth itself had shifted beneath his feet.

Slowly, he exhaled, straightened his shoulders, and spoke.

"We do not know what tomorrow will bring," he admitted. "But what we do know is that we are strong. We have faced worse, and we endure. We do not lead with fear. We lead with faith—in ourselves, in each other."

Silence stretched for a moment. Then, a warrior nodded. Another gripped his spear tighter, hope rekindled in his eyes.

Marcus felt something stir within him.

Leadership was not about having all the answers. It was about standing firm, even when the path was unclear.

And that was enough.

Returning With Clarity

With a sharp inhale, Marcus was back.

The firelight faded, replaced by the soft glow of Clara's lamp. His heart still pounded as if he had truly stood before his people in the jungle, as if the weight of their expectations had been his own.

And maybe... it had been.

Clara studied his face. "What did you see?"

Marcus exhaled, rubbing a hand over his face. "A leader. A chief. He had no answers, but he led anyway." He looked up, his voice steadier. "He was afraid, just like me."

Clara nodded. "Because doubt is part of leadership."

Marcus let the thought settle. "I've spent so much time thinking I needed to be certain about everything. That if I had doubts, it meant I wasn't fit to lead."

She smiled. "And now?"

He sat up straighter, something new—or perhaps something rediscovered—in his eyes.

"Now I understand. Leadership isn't about never questioning yourself. It's about moving forward despite the questions."

He stood, feeling lighter. The burden was still there, but it no longer felt impossible.

Before he left, he turned to Clara. "Thank you."

She simply nodded. "Lead well, Marcus."

And he would.

This time, without fear.

The Fourth Seeker: An Artist's Block

Sophie sat in her dimly lit studio, staring at the blank canvas before her. The brushes, once extensions of her soul, now felt foreign in her hands. The colours in her paints had lost their vibrancy.

She let out a sigh, rubbing her temples. Nothing. No inspiration, no passion—just an empty void where her creativity had once thrived.

Clara watched her for a moment before setting the Book of Echoes on the table between them.

Sophie glanced at it warily. "What is this?"

Clara smiled. "A mirror. A doorway. A reminder."

Sophie hesitated, but something in Clara's tone—gentle yet certain—made her reach forward.

The moment her fingertips touched the cover, the world shifted.

The Artisan's Rebellion

Sophie found herself in a small, dimly lit workshop, the scent of clay and burning wood filling the air. A woman sat at a worktable; her hands stained with pigment as she carefully carved intricate symbols into a ceramic vase.

Sophie could feel the artisan's heartbeat—steady, yet defiant.

The door creaked open. A man in foreign armour entered, his gaze sweeping the room with suspicion. Sophie felt the artisan still, her chisel pausing mid-stroke.

"Show me your work," the man demanded.

The artisan wiped her hands and lifted a seemingly ordinary plate, its designs simple, traditional. The soldier glanced at it, grunted in approval, and left without another word.

But the moment the door shut, the artisan let out a breath—and turned over the true piece she had been working on.

Hidden beneath the surface were forbidden symbols—messages of resilience, resistance, hope.

Sophie's breath caught. The artisan had not been creating for beauty alone. She had been fighting—in silence, through art, through the defiance of creation itself.

Even when the world tried to erase her culture, she carved it back into existence.

The realization crashed over Sophie like a wave.

Art was not just expression. It was survival.

The Canvas Speaks Again

With a sharp gasp, Sophie returned.

The dim studio came into focus. Her breath was unsteady, her hands trembling—not with fear, but with understanding.

Clara watched her carefully. "What did you see?"

Sophie swallowed; her throat dry. "She created because she had to. Because if she didn't, her people's stories would be erased."

Clara nodded. "And what does that mean for you?"

Sophie turned to her empty canvas. It was no longer empty. She could already see the strokes, the colours, the unspoken words waiting to be painted.

Her voice was quiet, but sure. "That I've been looking for inspiration in the wrong place."

She picked up a brush, dipped it into the paint, and began.

Not to impress. Not too perfect.

But to speak.

Echoes of Transformation

As Clara guided each seeker through the Book of Echoes, she saw the profound transformations unfold before her eyes.

Marcus, once paralyzed by doubt, now led with both strength and humility.

Elena, consumed by grief, found purpose in honouring her child through compassion.

Sophie, lost in artistic silence, rediscovered her voice through the power of creation.

Each of them had stepped into the past, not to escape their struggles, but to understand them—to carry forward the lessons of those who came before.

Clara closed the book gently, a quiet reverence in her heart.

Because in the echoes of history lay not just the past, but the keys to healing, purpose, and evolution.

The Book of Echoes Finds Another Way

Chapter Seventeen: The Forgotten Name

London, 1893.

The gas lamps flickered in the thick London fog as Margaret Lovell tightened her coat against the chill. The city streets were alive with whispers—cobbled alleys echoing with the clatter of carriage wheels, the murmur of merchants, the faint chime of church bells lost in the smog.

But Margaret heard something else.

Something older.

Something calling.

She had felt it for weeks—a strange pull, an invisible thread winding through the fabric of her mind. It had started with dreams.

Visions of a book.

A book she had never seen, yet somehow remembered.

She had spent every night searching—through archives, through forgotten texts in the dim-lit corners of the British Museum's library. But no matter how many pages she turned, she never found it.

Because it did not exist on any shelf.

Not yet.

Chapter Eighteen: The Bookshop on Fleet Street

It was on a Tuesday that Margaret found the book.

Or rather, that it found her.

She had been wandering aimlessly, lost in thought, when she saw the flickering candlelight inside a narrow bookshop tucked between two larger buildings. The kind of shop that shouldn't have been there—the kind no one remembered until they needed it.

She pushed open the heavy wooden door, and a small bell chimed overhead. The scent of old parchment and ink filled her lungs, familiar yet foreign.

Behind the counter, an old man with silver-rimmed spectacles looked up. His gaze was knowing, as if he had been expecting her.

Margaret hesitated. "I—" She stopped, uncertain of why she was even here.

The man simply nodded and turned away, disappearing into the maze of towering bookshelves.

Margaret followed.

Through narrow corridors of forgotten knowledge, past dust-covered books filled with languages she couldn't read. Until, at last, he stopped before a lone wooden pedestal.

And there, resting on its surface, was the book.

A leather-bound book, its cover unmarked, as though its title had long since faded from time itself.

Margaret reached out, her fingers barely brushing its surface. The world cracked apart.

Chapter Nineteen: A Life Once Lived

She was falling.

Through time. Through memory. Through herself.

The fog of London disappeared, replaced by the scent of salt and damp earth. The flickering gas lamps faded into torchlight.

She was no longer in 1893.

She was someone else.

She opened her eyes and found herself standing on the edge of a towering cliffside, waves crashing violently below.

Her hands were bloodstained.

And behind her, a voice called out—a voice filled with grief, anger, betrayal.

"Margaret!"

She turned. And she remembered everything.

Chapter Twenty: The Buried Past

It happened centuries ago.

A different name. A different life.

She had lived and died on this very cliff.

She had been the daughter of a noble house, accused of treason against the crown. But the truth had been buried—only she had known what really happened.

And someone had made sure she never spoke of it again.

Someone had pushed her.

Sent her tumbling into the ocean, her last breath stolen by the waves.

And now, she was here again.

The book had not brought her back to relive the moment.

It had brought her back to understand it.

She had not been weak. She had not been a victim.

She had been silenced.

And for lifetimes, that silence had followed her.

It was why, even in 1893, she had always felt unseen.

Why she had never truly found her voice.

Until now.

Chapter Twenty-One: The Guardian's Choice

Margaret woke with a gasp.

She was back in the bookshop.

The old man watched her, his face unreadable.

"The book does not show us what we wish to see," he said at last. "Only what we must."

Margaret's hands trembled, the memory of the cliffside still fresh, as though the salt water clung to her skin.

"I—" she swallowed. "I was murdered."

The old man nodded. "And now, you remember."

She looked down at the book, still resting before her.

She had spent lifetimes running from the truth. But now she understood.

The book did not just reveal the past.

It healed it.

And with that knowledge, a new understanding settled over her.

This was not just her journey.

She was not the only one who had forgotten.

And if she could remember, she could help others do the same.

Margaret closed the book.

And when she looked up, the old man was gone.

The bookshop was empty.

And in her hands, the book had become hers.

She was no longer just a seeker.

She was the next guardian.

And the journey had only just begun.

Epilogue: The Threads of Time

Elsewhere, in another time, in another place...

A new seeker was awakening. The book had begun calling to someone else. And the cycle would begin again.

Because time is not a river, it is a circle. And some echoes never fade.

A New Seeker; A Different Time

Chapter Twenty-Two: The Astronaut and the Book

Year: 2147

Location: Lunar Colony, Mare Serenitatis

The stars stretched endlessly above Dr. Kieran Voss; a silent ocean of darkness interrupted only by the glowing Earth far in the distance. He stood at the observation deck of Lunar Base ECHO-7, the glass panel before him revealing the barren beauty of the Moon's surface.

For months, he had been having dreams.

Visions of places he had never been. Voices speaking in languages he did not know, yet understood. A name—one that did not belong to him, yet felt like his own.

And most of all, a book.

A book that did not exist in any archive, any database, or any historical record.

Until today.

Because it had appeared.

Not on Earth. Not in a museum.

But here, on the Moon.

Chapter Twenty-Three: The Artifact

It had been a routine excavation. The research team had been scanning an ancient lunar crater, searching for signs of deep-space matter when the scanners picked up something impossible.

A structure.

Buried beneath the Moon's surface.

A door that had no right to exist.

Kieran had led the investigation, unsure if what they had found was human-made or something... else. But when the excavation revealed the book, everything changed.

No oxygen. No life. No reason why it should be here, perfectly preserved in an airless vacuum.

Yet there it was.

Bound in leather that looked untouched by time, its pages filled with words that shifted and changed when he tried to read them.

And the moment he touched it—

He fell through time.

Chapter Twenty-Four: The Fall Through Memory

The sterile walls of the lunar base vanished.

The hum of machinery, the weightlessness of low gravity—gone.

Kieran's body plummeted through space, through light and darkness, through the unseen corridors of time itself.

Until his feet hit the ground.

And he opened his eyes to a battlefield.

Chapter Twenty-Five: The Soldier He Once Was

The air was thick with smoke. The sky burned red.

Kieran stood in the middle of a war he did not recognize, but somehow knew intimately.

The weight of armour pressed against his body. A sword—not a laser tool, not a mechanical instrument, but a crude, bloodstained blade—was clutched in his hand.

And around him, men screamed.

The clash of metal. The scent of death.

This was Earth, but not the Earth he had known.

This was the 10th century.

And he had been a warrior.

Flashes of memory hit him like an explosion—

A kingdom at war. A battle fought for a cause long forgotten.

And a betrayal that had cost him his life.

"You were the commander," a voice whispered, echoing through the battlefield.

Kieran turned.

A soldier stood before him, helmet cracked, blood running down his face. His eyes burned with rage and sorrow.

"You led us here. You led us to die."

The guilt hit Kieran like a knife to the chest.

Because he remembered.

He had ordered the charge. He had believed in victory.

And instead, they had all perished.

He had perished.

And now, over a thousand years later, the book had brought him back.

To face it. To understand. To heal.

Chapter Twenty-Six: The Choice That Was Never Made

The battle raged around him, but Kieran no longer felt like just a soldier.

He was both the past and the present, trapped between who he had been and who he had become.

And suddenly, he saw it—

A single moment in time. The moment before the charge. The moment before he doomed them all.

"What if you had chosen differently?" the voice whispered again.

For centuries, for lifetimes, he had carried the guilt of this war.

But now, he was being given the chance to change it.

Kieran inhaled sharply.

Then, for the first time in a thousand years, he spoke the words he had never spoken:

"Hold the line. Do not charge."

And the world shattered.

Chapter Twenty-Seven: The Awakening

Kieran's eyes snapped open. He was back.

Back in the lunar base, back beneath the artificial lights, the oxygen thrusters humming softly in the walls.

The book rested in his hands.

Only now, the cover had changed.

No longer blank, it bore a single inscription.

His name.

Kieran exhaled, his body shaking. He had been so sure the visions were just fragments of his imagination. But now, he knew the truth.

The book did not belong to the past.

It existed outside of time, waiting for those who needed it, revealing the wounds buried deep in the fabric of the soul.

And he was not the first to find it.

Others had held it before him.

Others would hold it after him.

But for now, in this moment, in the year 2147, on the surface of a dead moon,

It was his.

Epilogue: The Next Guardian

Kieran sat alone in the observation deck, staring at the Earth as it hung in the void.

The book lay open before him, its pages blank.

Waiting.

He was not just an astronaut anymore.

He was not just a scientist.

He was a seeker.

And soon, just as it had called to him, it would call to another.

Because time is not linear.

It is a circle.

And some stories are never truly finished.

Only waiting to be remembered.

Another Seeker, Another Time

Chapter Twenty-Eight: The Samurai and the Book

Kyoto, Japan — Year 1602

The cherry blossoms were in full bloom as Hana Ishikawa knelt beside the koi pond in her family's garden. The wind carried the scent of spring, rustling through the silk of her kimono.

Yet despite the beauty surrounding her, she could not shake the unease curling in her chest.

For weeks, she had been plagued by visions— strange and impossible memories of battles she had never fought, of swords clashing in the dead of night, of blood staining her hands.

But the strangest of all was the book.

A book she had never seen, yet felt as though it had always been with her.

And today, it arrived.

Wrapped in fine silk, an unmarked leather-bound book had been left outside her chamber door with no explanation, no sender.

Only a single note tucked within its pages:

"It is time to remember."

Her hands trembled as she turned the first page.

And in an instant, her world shattered.

Chapter Twenty-Nine: The Warrior She Once Was

Hana fell.

Through darkness. Through memory.

Through time.

When she opened her eyes, she was no longer in Kyoto.

She was standing in the middle of a battlefield.

Her body was different—stronger, armoured, poised for battle. The weight of a katana pressed into her palm. The sound of war drums pounded in her ears.

She was no longer Hana Ishikawa, daughter of a noble house.

She was Takeo, a samurai warrior, and this was the night he would die.

Chapter Thirty: The Last Stand

Hana's mind screamed in confusion, but her body remembered.

She knew how to move, how to fight.

Knew the men standing beside her, warriors sworn to the same cause, their faces twisted in grim determination.

This was the Siege of Osaka.

And she—he—had fought for the wrong side.

The enemy forces outnumbered them five to one. The battle was already lost.

But they had fought anyway.

Because that was the samurai way.

Because Takeo had sworn to die with honour.

But as Hana stood there, trapped in his body, watching the enemy descend like a black wave, a single thought pierced through the chaos:

"What if I had lived?"

She had always accepted this fate in the past.

But now, centuries later, the book had brought her back for a reason.

To change the story.

Chapter Thirty-One: Breaking the Cycle

The enemy charged.

Takeo's men braced for death.

But Hana did something different.

She dropped her sword.

The warriors beside her gasped. The enemy hesitated.

And at that moment, she spoke.

"Enough," she said.

And for the first time in any lifetime, Takeo did not fight to die.

He fought to survive.

Chapter Thirty-Two: The Return

Hana gasped as she was pulled back.

The battlefield vanished. The past faded into the wind.

She was kneeling once again beside the koi pond, the book resting in her lap.

Only now, she understood.

She had spent lifetimes believing that honour meant dying for a cause.

But today, she broke the cycle.

Honor was not in death.

It was in choosing to live.

And now, she was free

Chapter Thirty-Three: The Path of the Book

The book was still open.

But its pages were blank.

Waiting.

She had rewritten her past. And now, like those before her, she knew the truth—

This book was not just hers.

It was a gateway.

A path through time, meant for those ready to face the echoes of their past.

And somewhere, in another time, in another place—

It was calling to someone new.

A New Seeker in the Industrial Age

Chapter Thirty-Four: The Engineer and the Book

Manchester, England — Year 1851

The air was thick with the soot of progress as Thomas Whitaker navigated the bustling streets of Manchester. Steam-powered machines clattered in factories, and the hum of innovation was palpable. As a skilled engineer, Thomas was at the heart of this transformation, contributing to the marvels of the Industrial Revolution.

Yet, amidst the triumphs of engineering, he felt an inexplicable void—a sense that something essential was missing. Lately, his nights were restless, haunted by vivid dreams of a mysterious book and a life he couldn't recall.

One evening, as he returned home, a peculiar package awaited him. Wrapped in aged parchment, it bore no sender's mark. Inside, he found an unmarked leather-bound book. His heart raced; this was the book from his dreams.

With trembling hands, Thomas opened it, and the world around him began to blur.

Chapter Thirty-Five: The Weaver's Tale

Thomas found himself in a dimly lit cottage, the rhythmic clanking of a loom filling the space. He looked down to see calloused hands deftly weaving threads—a stark contrast to his usual ink-stained fingers.

He was no longer an engineer but a weaver in the early 18th century. The realization hit him hard; this was a past life.

Memories flooded back: the struggle to make ends meet, the encroachment of mechanized looms threatening his craft, and the despair of obsolescence. He had led a rebellion against the machines, believing they would destroy livelihoods.

But the rebellion had failed, leading to his arrest and execution. His final thoughts were of regret—not for his actions, but for not embracing change.

Chapter Thirty-Six: Embracing Transformation

Back in his own time, Thomas awoke with a start, the book still in his lap. The experience had been more than a dream; it was a revelation.

He realized that his unease stemmed from a deep-seated fear of change—a remnant from his past life. The Industrial Revolution, with all its advancements, was a double-edged sword, and he had once been on the opposing side.

Determined to break the cycle, Thomas resolved to approach his work with empathy, considering the societal impacts of technological progress. He would advocate for the fair treatment of workers and the responsible implementation of new technologies.

The book had shown him that while innovation drives society forward, it must be balanced with compassion and foresight.

Epilogue: The Ever-Turning Wheel

The book had once again found its seeker, bridging past and present to impart timeless lessons.

As Thomas embraced his newfound purpose, the book quietly vanished, awaiting the next soul in need of its wisdom.

For in the grand tapestry of existence, each thread is connected, and the wheel of time turns unceasingly, guiding seekers toward understanding and growth.

A New Seeker in the Digital Revolution

Chapter Thirty-seven: The Programmer and the Book

Silicon Valley, USA — Year 1999

The air buzzed with anticipation as the world approached the new millennium. Emily Chen, a talented software developer, was at the forefront of the digital revolution, working tirelessly to prepare systems for the Y2K transition. The fear of the millennium bug loomed large, threatening to disrupt global infrastructures.

Late one evening, as Emily sifted through lines of code, she received an anonymous package. Inside was an unmarked, leather-bound book—a stark contrast to her digital world. Curiosity piqued, she opened it, and the room seemed to warp around her.

Chapter Thirty-eight: The Telegraph Operator's Dilemma

Emily found herself in a dimly lit room, the rhythmic clicking of a telegraph machine filling the air. She looked down to see her hands deftly tapping out messages in Morse code. The calendar on the wall read 1876.

She was now Samuel, a telegraph operator during the dawn of the telephone era. The invention of the telephone threatened to render his skills obsolete, and he faced a choice:

Embrace the new technology, learning and adapting to the changing landscape.

Cling to the familiar, resisting change and potentially facing obsolescence.

Samuel had chosen the latter, leading to a life of hardship and regret.

Chapter Thirty-nine: Embracing Change

Back in her office, Emily awoke with a start, the book resting on her desk. The experience had been more than a dream; it was a revelation.

She realized that her resistance to emerging technologies, driven by fear of the unknown, mirrored Samuel's plight. Determined not to repeat past mistakes, Emily resolved to:

Embrace new innovations, staying ahead of technological advancements.

Foster a culture of continuous learning, encouraging her team to adapt and grow.

Balance caution with curiosity, ensuring responsible development and implementation.

The book had shown her that while technology evolves, the human response to change remains constant.

Epilogue: The Ever-Turning Wheel

The book had once again found its seeker, bridging past and present to impart timeless lessons.

As Emily embraced her newfound perspective, the book quietly vanished, awaiting the next soul in need of its wisdom.

For in the grand tapestry of existence, each thread is connected, and the wheel of time turns unceasingly, guiding seekers toward understanding and growth.

Chapter forty: The Spy and the Book

Berlin, Germany — Year 1942

The city was a ghost of its former self, its streets cloaked in fear and secrecy. The world was at war, and behind every shadow lurked a whisper of betrayal. Julian Cross had learned to survive in the spaces between those whispers.

He was a British intelligence officer, embedded deep within enemy territory, masquerading as a loyal German officer. His mission was clear—uncover the Reich's deepest secrets and ensure they never reached the battlefield.

But secrets had a way of finding him first.

One cold evening, hidden beneath the dim light of his candle lit desk, he found an unmarked package among the coded messages delivered to his safe house. It bore no insignia, no sender—only his name, scrawled in a hand that sent a chill through him.

Inside, wrapped in aged parchment, was a leather-bound book.

It was impossible. He had seen this book before, in his dreams.

Chapter Forty-One: A Life He Shouldn't Remember

The moment Julian opened the book, his vision blurred. The candlelight flickered. The walls of his safe house dissolved.

Then—he was falling.

The cold night of Berlin vanished, replaced by the roaring heat of another war.

When he hit the ground, his boots splashed in blood.

His hands gripped a sword, not a gun.

The sounds of cannon fire and muskets rang in his ears, but they did not belong to this war.

Because this was France, and the year was 1793.

Chapter Forty-Two: The Guillotine's Shadow

He stood in a crowded square, the sky grey with smoke. The air reeked of sweat, fear, and revolution. The guillotine loomed ahead, its blade sharp, dripping with the weight of history.

Julian's breath hitched. He knew this place.

Because in this life, he was not Julian Cross.

He was Étienne Beaumont, a nobleman accused of treason against the Republic. And today, he would die beneath that blade.

The memories came in sharp flashes:

A woman with piercing green eyes, whispering his name as she betrayed him to the revolutionaries.

Gold coins changing hands, sealing his fate.

His last words, spoken in defiance before they dragged him to the executioner's stage.

He had trusted her.

And she had sent him to his death.

Just as someone in his present life was about to do the same.

Chapter Forty-Three: The Message Across Time

Julian gasped, snapping back into his body. The guillotine disappeared. The French Revolution was gone.

He was back in 1942. Back in Berlin.

The book lay open before him, its pages still turning.

Sweat beaded on his brow as realization hit him. This was not just a memory. It was a warning. In his past life, he had trusted the wrong person and died for it.

And now, in this war, in this mission, history was about to repeat itself.

Someone in his network—someone he trusted—was about to betray him.

But this time...

This time, he had the book. This time, he had a chance to change the ending.

Chapter Forty-Four: The Spy's Next Move

Julian's pulse thundered as he closed the book. He no longer saw it as a relic.

It was a weapon.

A bridge between past and present, warning him of the mistakes he was doomed to repeat.

The book had saved him.

Now, he had one night to uncover the traitor before they uncovered him.

One night before the executioner's blade fell again.

And this time...

He refused to die.

Julian's Race Against Time

Chapter Forty-Five: The Web of Deceit

Berlin's streets lay under a thick veil of darkness, the oppressive silence broken only by the distant hum of military vehicles. Julian Cross, his mind still reeling from the revelations of the mysterious book, knew that every second counted. The spectre of betrayal loomed large, and he was determined to unmask the traitor before they sealed his fate.

His clandestine network within the city was vast, comprising informants, double agents, and unsuspecting civilians. Yet, the book's haunting vision had narrowed his suspicions to a select few. He meticulously reviewed recent intelligence reports, cross-referencing them with intercepted communications. Patterns began to emerge—subtle inconsistencies, delayed transmissions, and coded messages that hinted at duplicity.

One name resurfaced repeatedly: Klaus Heller, a high-ranking Abwehr officer who had recently been integrated into Julian's operations. Heller's credentials were impeccable, his loyalty ostensibly unwavering. However, the book's revelation had cast a shadow of doubt over him.

Chapter Forty-Six: The Confrontation

Under the guise of routine protocol, Julian arranged a midnight rendezvous with Heller in a secluded warehouse on the city's outskirts. The location was deliberately chosen—isolated, with no potential for eavesdropping.

As Heller arrived, his demeanour was calm, almost too composed. The two men exchanged formalities before delving into operational discussions. Julian, employing his training in psychological manipulation, subtly steered the conversation towards recent security breaches.

"It's disconcerting," Julian mused aloud, "how our enemies always seem one step ahead. Almost as if someone within our ranks is feeding them information."

Heller's eyes flickered momentarily—a barely perceptible sign, but enough to confirm Julian's suspicions.

"Do you have any leads?" Heller inquired; his voice steady but with an undertone of apprehension.

"Perhaps," Julian replied, locking eyes with him. "But trust is a fragile thing, easily shattered by betrayal."

The tension was palpable. Heller's facade began to crack, beads of sweat forming on his brow. In a swift motion, Julian drew his sidearm, aiming it squarely at Heller.

"It's over, Klaus. The game is up."

Heller's shoulders slumped, a resigned sigh escaping his lips. "You were always astute, Julian. It's a pity our paths converged this way."

Chapter Forty-Seven: The Revelation

With Heller detained, Julian delved into his personal quarters, uncovering clandestine radio equipment and cipher codes linking him directly to the enemy. Among the incriminating evidence was a photograph of Heller with a woman—the same woman from Julian's vision, the one who had betrayed him in a past life.

The realisation was staggering. The book had not only unveiled the betrayal but had also illuminated the intricate web of connections transcending time. The past and present were intertwined in a dance of fate and destiny.

Chapter Forty-Eight: The Aftermath

With the traitor exposed, Julian fortified his network, implementing stringent protocols to prevent future infiltrations. The book remained his enigmatic guide, its pages now blank, awaiting the next seeker in need of its wisdom.

As Berlin continued to smoulder under the ravages of war, Julian understood that his journey was far from over. The echoes of the past had provided clarity, but the future remains uncertain. With renewed resolve, he prepared to face the challenges ahead, knowing that the lessons of history would guide his path.

A New Seeker in the Age of Exploration

Chapter Forty-Nine: The Navigator and the Book

Lisbon, Portugal — Year 1492

The harbour of Lisbon was a tapestry of sails and masts, ships arriving and departing to the farthest reaches of the known world. The scent of saltwater mingled with exotic spices, hinting at lands beyond the horizon. Among the throng of sailors and merchants stood Isabella de Avila, a young navigator with a thirst for discovery that defied the conventions of her time.

Isabella had always felt the pull of the unknown, a magnetic attraction to the mysteries that lay beyond the mapped edges of the world. Her father, a respected cartographer, had nurtured her curiosity, teaching her the art of navigation and the science of the stars. Yet, as a woman, her aspirations were often met with scepticism and derision.

One evening, as she pored over sea charts in her modest quarters, a knock echoed through the wooden door. Opening it, she found no one—only a weathered, leather-bound book resting on the threshold. Its cover bore no title, but an inexplicable familiarity drew her to it.

Curiosity piqued; Isabella opened the book. The pages were filled with intricate illustrations of celestial maps and annotations in a script she couldn't decipher. As her fingers traced the delicate lines, a sensation of vertigo overcame her, and the room seemed to dissolve around her.

Chapter Fifty: The Viking's Voyage

When the dizziness subsided, Isabella found herself standing on the deck of a sturdy wooden ship, the chill of the northern wind biting at her skin. The crew around her spoke in a guttural language, their attire and demeanour foreign yet oddly familiar.

She realised, with a mix of awe and disbelief, that she had been transported into the body of a Viking navigator during the 9th century. The ship was part of a fleet sailing into uncharted waters, driven by a desire to discover new lands and wealth.

As days turned into weeks, Isabella—now living as the Viking navigator—experienced the exhilaration and perils of exploration. They encountered treacherous storms, navigated by the stars, and finally sighted a verdant coastline—the shores of what would later be known as Iceland.

Throughout the journey, she grappled with the challenges of leadership, the weight of decision-making, and the constant tension between ambition and responsibility. These experiences resonated deeply with her own aspirations and the obstacles she faced in her era.

Chapter Fifty-One: The Return

Abruptly, Isabella was pulled back to her own time, the familiar surroundings of her quarters materializing around her. The book lay open before her, its pages now blank, as if the ink had faded into the ether.

The vividness of the experience left her breathless. It was more than a dream; it was a revelation. The courage and determination of the Viking navigator mirrored her own desires and fears. The journey had imparted lessons that transcended time—about leadership, exploration, and the resilience needed to overcome societal constraints.

Empowered by this newfound wisdom, Isabella resolved to pursue her ambitions with renewed vigor. She would petition for a commission to lead an expedition, armed with the knowledge that the spirit of exploration was a timeless endeavour, unbound by gender or era.

The mysterious book had bridged the chasm of centuries, connecting her to a kindred spirit from the past. Its purpose fulfilled, it vanished without a trace, leaving Isabella with a profound sense of purpose and a destiny intertwined with the echoes of history.

Chapter Fifty-Two: The Philosopher's Revelation

Paris, France — Year 1775

In the heart of Paris, during a time when reason and science began to challenge long-held beliefs, lived Étienne Moreau, a philosopher deeply engrossed in the pursuit of knowledge. The city buzzed with intellectual fervour, salons filled with debates on liberty, progress, and the rights of man.

One evening, as Étienne perused ancient manuscripts in a dimly lit library, he discovered a peculiar, leather-bound book nestled among the dusty tomes. Its cover bore no title, yet it emanated an inexplicable allure. Drawn to its mystery, he opened it to find pages filled with symbols and scripts unlike any he had seen.

As he delved deeper, the room around him seemed to fade, and he was enveloped by a cascade of visions—glimpses of distant lands, unfamiliar faces, and events spanning epochs. The experience was overwhelming, yet profoundly enlightening.

Chapter Fifty-Three The Alchemist's Journey

Emerging from the visions, Étienne found himself in the body of an alchemist during the 9th century in the heart of Baghdad, the epicentre of the Islamic Golden Age. Surrounded by scholars and scientists, he was amidst a civilization that cherished knowledge and discovery.

In this new existence, Étienne, as the alchemist, engaged in experiments to transmute base metals into gold and sought the elusive elixir of life. Through his studies, he uncovered principles of chemistry and medicine far ahead of his original time. He grappled with the ethical implications of his pursuits, understanding that true enlightenment transcended material gain.

These experiences instilled in him a profound appreciation for the interconnectedness of all knowledge and the enduring quest for understanding that transcends cultures and eras.

Chapter Fifty-four: The Enlightened Path

Abruptly, Étienne was drawn back to his own time, the familiar surroundings of the Parisian library reappearing. The mysterious book lay before him, its pages now blank, as if the visions had been absorbed into his consciousness.

The journey had imparted invaluable insights. He realised that the pursuit of knowledge was a universal endeavour, unbounded by time or place. The alchemist's dedication mirrored his own, and the ethical considerations of their quests were strikingly similar.

Empowered by this revelation, Étienne dedicated himself to fostering a spirit of inquiry and openness. He began writing treatises that emphasised the unity of knowledge and the importance of ethical considerations in scientific pursuits. His works encouraged collaboration across disciplines and cultures, advocating for a holistic approach to understanding the world.

The mystical book had once again bridged time and space, guiding a seeker toward wisdom that would illuminate the path for future generations. Its purpose fulfilled, it vanished from the library, awaiting the next soul in need of its timeless guidance.

Chapter Fifty-Five: The Patriot's Awakening

Boston, Massachusetts — Year 1775

The air was thick with anticipation in the bustling port city of Boston. Tensions between the American colonies and the British Crown had reached a boiling point, and whispers of revolution echoed through the cobblestone streets. In a modest study, illuminated by the flickering glow of a solitary candle, sat Samuel Prescott, a dedicated physician and fervent patriot.

Late into the night, as Samuel pored over medical texts, a peculiar sensation washed over him. His gaze was irresistibly drawn to an unassuming, leather-bound book nestled among his collection—a book he did not recall acquiring. Its cover bore no title, yet it emanated an aura of profound significance.

Compelled by an inexplicable force, Samuel opened the book. The pages were filled with intricate diagrams and writings in a script both foreign and familiar. As his fingers traced the delicate lines, a sudden vertigo overtook him, and the room dissolved into darkness.

Chapter Fifty-Six: The Spartan's Trial

When clarity returned, Samuel found himself in an entirely different world. He stood amidst a rugged landscape, clad in bronze armour, a heavy shield strapped to his arm. The air was filled with the distant clamour of battle. He realised, with a mix of awe and trepidation, that he had assumed the identity of a Spartan warrior in ancient Greece, circa 480 BCE.

The Spartans were preparing to confront the Persian forces at the Battle of Thermopylae. As he trained and strategized alongside his fellow warriors, Samuel experienced first-hand the discipline, camaraderie, and unwavering resolve that defined Spartan society. He grappled with the harsh realities of war, the concept of sacrifice for the greater good, and the stark contrast between individual desires and collective duty.

These experiences resonated deeply with Samuel, mirroring the burgeoning revolutionary spirit in his own time. The Spartans' valour and commitment to their cause provided him with profound insights into leadership, resilience, and the complexities of freedom.

Chapter Fifty-Seven: The Midnight Ride

Abruptly, Samuel was pulled back to his own era, the familiar surroundings of his study materialising around him. The mysterious book lay open before him, its pages now blank, as if the knowledge it imparted had been absorbed into his very being.

The vividness of the experience left him breathless. It was more than a dream; it was a revelation. The lessons from his time as a Spartan warrior illuminated his path forward. He understood the importance of unity, courage, and strategic foresight in the face of overwhelming odds.

Empowered by this newfound wisdom, Samuel became more than just a physician; he emerged as a pivotal figure in the fight for independence. He joined forces with fellow patriots, including Paul Revere and William Dawes, in their daring midnight rides to warn of the approaching British forces. His actions galvanized the colonial militia, contributing to the battles of Lexington and Concord, and igniting the flames of revolution.

The enigmatic book had once again bridged time and space, imparting timeless wisdom to a seeker poised at a pivotal moment in history. Its purpose fulfilled, it vanished without a trace, awaiting the next soul in need of its guidance.

Chapter Fifty-Eight: The Guardian's Revelation

In the ethereal realm beyond the constraints of time and space, there exists a being of profound wisdom and eternal presence—the Guardian of the Book of Echoes. This ancient custodian has watched over the mystical book since its inception, ensuring that its profound knowledge reaches those destined to guide humanity toward enlightenment.

The Guardian resides in a sanctum of light and shadow, a place where the past, present, and future converge. From this vantage point, they observe the tapestry of human history, identifying pivotal moments and individuals whose actions can alter the course of destiny.

Throughout the ages, the Guardian has facilitated the Book's journey, guiding it to seekers such as Enheduanna, Hypatia, and Geoffrey Loveday. Each encounter was meticulously orchestrated to impart wisdom and inspire transformative change.

Now, as the world stands on the brink of unprecedented challenges and opportunities, the Guardian senses the emergence of a new seeker—one whose journey will intertwine with the legacy of the Book in unforeseen ways.

With a gesture, the Guardian summons the Book of Echoes, its pages shimmering with untold possibilities. The time has come to guide the next soul, to continue the eternal mission of enlightenment and healing.

Chapter Fifty-Nine: The Awakening

In the heart of modern-day London, amidst the ceaseless hum of city life, resides Dr. Eleanor "Ellie" Thompson, a renowned neuroscientist dedicated to unravelling the mysteries of the human mind. Despite her professional success, Ellie has been plagued by recurring dreams—vivid, haunting visions of places and people she has never known, yet that feel intimately familiar.

One evening, as a torrential rain batters the city, Ellie seeks refuge in a quaint, antiquarian bookstore tucked away in a narrow alley of Bloomsbury. Drawn to a secluded corner, her eyes fall upon an unassuming, leather-bound volume—the Book of Echoes. Its cover is worn, its pages yellowed with age, yet it emanates an inexplicable allure.

Compelled by an unseen force, Ellie opens the book. As her fingers trace the faded script, a sudden wave of vertigo overwhelms her, and the world around her dissolves into darkness

Chapter Sixty: The Ancestral Memory

When Ellie regains her senses, she finds herself in a vast, open plain under a sky painted with the hues of dawn. She is no longer in London but in a prehistoric landscape, surrounded by a tribe of early humans. To her astonishment, she understands their language and customs as if they were her own.

Immersed in this ancient world, Ellie experiences life through the eyes of a young tribal healer. She learns their methods of herbal medicine, their rituals, and their deep connection to the natural world. She witnesses their joys, sorrows, and the communal bonds that hold them together.

Through these experiences, Ellie realises that the emotions and sensations she is encountering mirror the inexplicable feelings and dreams she has had in her modern life. She begins to understand that these are not mere fantasies but ancestral memories encoded within her very being.

Chapter Sixty-One: The Revelation

Abruptly, Ellie is pulled back to the present, the dim light of the bookstore coming into focus. The Book of Echoes lies open before her, its pages now blank, as if the knowledge it imparted has been absorbed into her consciousness.

The experience leaves her breathless. She comprehends that the visions she has been experiencing are ancestral memories, echoes of lives lived long ago, imprinted within her DNA. This revelation aligns seamlessly with the principles of The Loveday Method, a therapeutic approach that facilitates mental time travel to access hidden memories responsible for generational trauma.

Empowered by this newfound understanding, Ellie embarks on a journey to integrate these ancestral insights into her work. She collaborates with practitioners of The Loveday Method, bridging the gap between neuroscience and ancestral memory retrieval. Together, they develop innovative therapies to help individuals confront and heal from generational traumas, unlocking the potential for profound personal transformation.

The Book of Echoes has once again fulfilled its purpose, guiding a seeker toward enlightenment and healing. As Ellie delves deeper into her research, she becomes a beacon of hope, illustrating the profound interconnectedness of all souls and the timeless quest for self-discovery.

A Meeting Across Time

Chapter Sixty-Two: The Convergence

In the heart of Alexandria, during the height of its intellectual splendour in 370 CE, the esteemed philosopher and mathematician Hypatia delved into the mysteries of the cosmos. One evening, as she studied the stars from her observatory, a peculiar sensation enveloped her—a feeling of being both present and elsewhere.

Simultaneously, in London, Dr. Eleanor "Ellie" Thompson, a neuroscientist in 2025, sat in her laboratory, analysing neural patterns associated with ancestral memories. Suddenly, she felt a strange connection, as if her consciousness was intertwining with another's across the fabric of time.

Chapter Sixty-Three the Dialogue Beyond Time

In a realm beyond the physical, where past and present converge, Hypatia and Ellie found themselves face-to-face.

Hypatia: "Greetings, traveller. By what means have we come to share this space?"

Ellie: "I... I'm not certain. One moment I was in my lab, and now I'm here, speaking with you. You seem familiar, as if from a distant memory."

Hypatia: "Perhaps the Book of Echoes has woven our paths together. I have encountered its wisdom, guiding my studies of the heavens and the principles of mathematics."

Ellie: "The Book of Echoes... I've read about it, a mystical book connecting seekers across time. Are you... Hypatia of Alexandria?"

Hypatia: "Indeed, I am. And you, traveller, from which era do you hail?"

Ellie: "I'm Dr. Ellie Thompson, from the year 2025. I'm a neuroscientist exploring how ancestral memories influence our present selves."

Hypatia: "Fascinating. It seems the Book has bridged our times to share knowledge. Tell me, what have you discovered in your studies?"

Ellie: "I've been developing a method to help individuals access and heal generational traumas encoded in their DNA. It's called The Loveday Method."

Hypatia: "A noble pursuit. In my time, I sought to understand the cosmos and our place within it. Perhaps our endeavours are more connected than they appear."

Ellie: "I believe so. Understanding the past can illuminate our present and guide our future. Your work laid the foundations for many scientific principles we now take for granted."

Hypatia: "And your work carries forward the quest for knowledge and healing. It seems the Book of Echoes has a purpose in uniting us—to show that the pursuit of wisdom is a timeless endeavour."

Chapter Sixty-Four: The Parting Gift

As their conversation deepened, both women felt a profound connection, transcending the boundaries of time. The realm around them began to waver, signalling the end of their encounter.

Hypatia: "Ellie, take with you the understanding that knowledge is a bridge across the ages. Our efforts, though separated by centuries, are part of a continuum."

Ellie: "Thank you, Hypatia. I will carry your wisdom into my work, knowing that we are all connected in this vast tapestry of existence."

With that, the convergence faded, and both returned to their respective times, forever changed by their encounter.

The Book of Echoes,

Having traversed various eras and guided numerous seekers, sensed a pivotal moment in its existence. Recognising the need for a more structured approach to aid humanity, the book returned to its Guardian, an ancient custodian entrusted with its safekeeping and purpose.

The Guardian, a timeless entity residing in a realm beyond the constraints of ordinary time, understood the profound significance of this return. The book's journeys had illuminated individual lives, but now it sought to influence humanity on a grander scale.

In communion with the Guardian, the book revealed its intent: to become a beacon of collective wisdom, accessible to all who earnestly sought understanding and enlightenment. No longer would it appear sporadically to isolated individuals; instead, it would manifest in forms comprehensible to different cultures and societies, embedding its essence in myths, legends, and teachings across the world.

Through this transformation, the Book of Echoes aimed to inspire a universal awakening, encouraging humanity to reflect on past lessons, recognise recurring patterns, and strive towards a harmonious future. The Guardian, honouring the book's evolved purpose, released it into the currents of human consciousness, allowing its echoes to resonate through the annals of history, guiding civilizations towards wisdom and unity.

Thus, the Book of Echoes transcended its physical form, becoming an eternal whisper in the collective human psyche, ever-present and ever-guiding, as humanity continued its journey through the ages.

Ancient Mystical Book

In the heart of a tranquil village, nestled between rolling hills and ancient forests, there existed a legend of a mystical book—a book said to possess the collective wisdom of the ancients. This book, it was whispered, had the power to guide chosen individuals toward profound discoveries that could heal the deepest wounds of humanity.

One fateful night, as the village lay under a canopy of twinkling stars, a young hypnoanalyst named Geoffrey Elliot Loveday was visited by a vivid dream. In this dream, the mystical book appeared before him, its pages glowing with an ethereal light. The book spoke to him without words, imparting a profound understanding of the human mind and the hidden traumas that traverse generations.

Upon awakening, Geoffrey felt an irresistible urge to write, despite never considering himself a writer. It was as if the book had unlocked a reservoir of knowledge within him. He began to develop a method that allowed individuals to journey back through time within their minds, to confront and heal from ancestral traumas affecting their present lives.

He named this transformative approach The Loveday Method. Through it, Geoffrey guided individuals into deep trances, leading them up a symbolic staircase to a door. Upon opening this door, they would traverse back to experiences from lives long past, uncovering and addressing the root causes of their current struggles.

The objective of this mystical encounter and the subsequent development of The Loveday Method was to provide a pathway for healing—bridging the past and present, and offering individuals the opportunity to release the invisible forces of generational trauma. Geoffrey's work illuminated the profound interconnectedness of all souls and the timeless quest for self-discovery and healing.

Thus, the mystical book's wisdom found its way into the modern world through Geoffrey, guiding humanity toward a deeper understanding of itself and the eternal bonds that unite us all.

This Is Just the Beginning

As Geoffrey Elliott Loveday, a professional hypnotherapist, hypnoanalyst, and certified hypnosis instructor, I have dedicated my career to exploring the depths of the human mind and facilitating healing through innovative techniques. My journey led me to develop the Loveday Method, a therapeutic approach that emerged from a profound dream, guiding clients to relive past lives and uncover emotions affecting their present well-being.

The Loveday Method is designed to take clients on a temporal journey, allowing them to experience lives lived long before their current existence. By accessing these deep-seated memories, individuals can identify and address emotional residues that manifest as challenges in their present lives. This process not only provides insight but also facilitates profound healing, enabling clients to release burdens they may have unconsciously carried across lifetimes.

Through my work, I have witnessed the transformative power of this method, as clients gain clarity, resolve deep-rooted issues, and achieve a sense of inner peace. The narratives and journeys presented in my writings aim to illustrate the profound impact of the Loveday Method, offering readers a glimpse into the possibilities of healing and self-discovery that lie within.

For those interested in exploring this therapeutic approach further, I offer training and resources through Mindlayers, where we delve into the intricacies of the Loveday Method and its application in hypnotherapy.

The Loveday Method stands as a testament to the profound connections between our past and present selves, offering a pathway to healing that transcends time and fosters holistic well-being.

Beyond Time: The Power to Revisit, Rewrite, and Heal

Imagine a world where time is not a barrier but a gateway—a place where the past isn't just remembered, but revisited. A world where every wound, every regret, every fractured piece of the soul can be mended, not by forgetting, but by returning.

You might call it fiction, a fantasy too impossible to be true. But what if it isn't? What if the journeys I have written are more than just stories? What if time can be unravelled, re-walked, re-written—not just in history books, but in the mind itself?

Think of the pain that lingers, the echoes of moments that haunt us. Now, imagine stepping back into those very moments, not as a prisoner, but as a healer. Imagine rewriting your own past, not by changing events, but by changing how they live within you.

This is not just a story. This is a truth waiting to be uncovered. And I am here to tell you—it is real.